Ruby Gloom®
#3 Staged Fright

By Rebecca McCarthy
Illustrated by Artful Doodlers

Grosset & Dunlap

GROSSET & DUNLAP
Published by the Penguin Group
Penguin Group (USA) Inc., 375 Hudson Street, New York, New York 10014, USA
Penguin Group (Canada), 90 Eglinton Avenue East, Suite 700, Toronto, Ontario M4P
2Y3, Canada (a division of Pearson Penguin Canada Inc.)
Penguin Books Ltd., 80 Strand, London WC2R 0RL, England
Penguin Group Ireland, 25 St. Stephen's Green, Dublin 2, Ireland
(a division of Penguin Books Ltd.)
Penguin Group (Australia), 250 Camberwell Road, Camberwell, Victoria 3124,
Australia (a division of Pearson Australia Group Pty. Ltd.)
Penguin Books India Pvt. Ltd., 11 Community Centre, Panchsheel Park, New Delhi—
110 017, India
Penguin Group (NZ), 67 Apollo Drive, Rosedale, North Shore 0632, New Zealand
(a division of Pearson New Zealand Ltd.)
Penguin Books (South Africa) (Pty.) Ltd., 24 Sturdee Avenue,
Rosebank, Johannesburg 2196, South Africa

Penguin Books Ltd., Registered Offices:
80 Strand, London WC2R 0RL, England

www.rubygloom.com

Library of Congress Control Number: 2008005245

ISBN 978-0-448-44850-3   10 9 8 7 6 5 4 3 2 1

Dear Friend,

Welcome to Gloomsville!

I'm Ruby Gloom, the happiest girl in the world, and I live in a wonderful old mansion with all of my friends. I can't wait for you to meet them. They mean the world to me.

There's Iris, a one-eyed girl who loves going on wild adventures; Skull Boy, who's always trying to figure out who's in his family tree; Frank and Len, brothers who share a body and a love of loud music; Poe, the smartest crow I know; Misery, a girl with the worst luck in the world; Scaredy Bat, a little bat who's afraid of everything; Boo Boo, a ghost who isn't the least bit scary; and Doom Kitty, my best friend.

My friends and I always find a way to have fun each and every day, no matter what obstacles stand in our way. In this story, Scaredy Bat had to overcome one of the biggest obstacles of all—fear. Luckily, he had his friends to help him . . . and one very special sock puppet!

Scaredy was pretty afraid of being alone in the dark, but like I always say, the bogeyman lives in the dark, so turn off the light and get to know him!

Your friend,

Ruby

Chapter One

"When it rains, it pours.
So grab an umbrella
and enjoy it!"

It was a very stormy morning in Gloomsville. Heavy, purple clouds hid the sun. The limbs of the trees swayed in the howling wind, and rain pounded into the ground, creating puddles and mudslides. Thunder clapped, lightning struck, and even though it was morning, the sky was still as dark as night.

Fair-skinned and freckle-faced Ruby Gloom was just waking up in her room on the top floor of the mansion. Slowly, she yawned and slipped out of bed. Approaching the window, still clutching her purple-heart-patterned blanket around her shoulders and rubbing her eyes, Ruby saw the large raindrops and muddy ground below. Her eyes opened wide and her mouth broke into a huge smile. "Oh goody!" she said excitedly, jumping up and down, "it's a rainy day!"

Ruby's exclamation woke up Doom Kitty, who had been sleeping in her small cat bed next to Ruby's nightstand. Doom snaked her tail over and lifted up one corner of her eye mask—just to see what all the fuss was about. When she saw the rain outside, she dropped the mask back into place and

covered her face with her paws. Cats don't like to get wet, and Doom Kitty was no exception. She sighed deeply and went back to sleep.

Tried to go back to sleep, that is. Ruby scooped her up and snuggled her hard. "Oh, Doom, I love it when everyone stays inside together and plays games all day. Let's go find the others and tell them the good news." Now wide awake, Doom Kitty nodded and then jumped to the ground. She groomed her midnight black fur while Ruby pulled on her orange-and-red-striped tights and black baby-doll dress. Ruby brushed her bright red hair, opened the door for Doom Kitty, and they both went out into the hallway.

At the top of the stairs, Iris was poised for takeoff. She sat on a chair that had two long wooden planks glued to the bottom of the legs, sort of like skis. Her single, violet-colored eye looked determinedly down the long, steep staircase. Her short, black hair was tucked tightly behind her ears. She held the banister with both arms, and just as Ruby and Doom turned the corner, she launched herself and the chair forward.

"Woo-hoo! I'm chair-skiing!" Iris shouted gleefully. Sure enough, the chair slid down the stairs smoothly, gradually gaining speed. But suddenly Iris hit a snag. The planks broke off  of the bottom of the chair, then the legs broke off, then the back broke off, until Iris was left holding on to nothing but the seat.

"Whoa!" she shouted, still thrilled by the ride. Iris was always looking for new and daring adventures. There was nothing she wouldn't try at least once.

She rode down the rest of the staircase until the very end, when the seat finally broke and she somersaulted to the floor in a spectacular crash landing. Ruby and Doom Kitty gasped at the loud crash, but then they heard Iris call out in her strong, spunky voice, "I'm good!"

Ruby and Doom hurried down the stairs.

"Hi, guys!" Iris said, brushing the dust off of her red-and-black dress. "Did you guys see the weather outside yet? It's fantastic—perfect mud for sledding down the biggest hill in Gloomsville!"

"That does sound like fun, but I'm not sure everyone will feel that way," Ruby said, chuckling.

"Maybe not," Iris said. "We can always do it

some other time. There will be plenty of rainy days to come!"

"Exactly. And today would be a wonderful day for an indoor adventure. Let's go find the others and decide which games we're going to play!" Ruby said enthusiastically, and the three of them skipped off toward Misery's basement room.

They knocked on the heavy lead door. Inside, they heard a muffled, raspy voice say, "Come in." Both Ruby and Iris had to push on the door with all their might to get it to budge, but finally it creaked open. They found Misery lying on her bed of nails, watching the spiders weave cobwebs in the corners of the ceiling. The rain outside must have found a crack in the roof, because small droplets of water leaked upon Misery's long, dark hair every few seconds. It figured that of all places, Misery's room would be the one with the leak in the ceiling. She always had the worst luck.

"Good morning, Misery," Ruby said quietly. "Ready to get up and have some fun?"

"It's raining," Misery said dryly. "Bad things happen to me when it rains."

"Yes, that's true," Ruby agreed, "but look on the bright side. Bad things happen to you when it doesn't rain. So what have you got to lose?"

Misery paused to consider the statement. Finally, she said, "That is an excellent point." She stood up to join her friends. Just as she took a step toward the door, the ceiling began to creak overhead.
Suddenly, the tiny leak turned into a very large leak, dumping rainwater all over Misery's head.

"Hmm," Misery murmured as she wrung out her hair, and then trudged forward.

She had taken about four steps when Skull Boy came barreling down the stairs and smacked right into Misery, who then fell to the ground. Skull Boy fell, too, and his bones scattered in every direction.

Skull Boy's bones came apart easily and often. But he usually didn't let it get him down—after all, his friends were always there to help put him back together.

"Here's your femur!" Iris said, snapping the thighbone in place between the kneecap and the hip bone.

"Ulna!" called Ruby, holding up a forearm bone.

"Humerus," said Misery. "The bone, not the adjective." And she grabbed the larger forearm bone and rose to her feet. In no time, they had Skull Boy in one piece again.

"Thanks!" he said. "Sorry I knocked you over, Misery. I guess there's no relation between me and the Great Farini."

"Who?" Misery asked.

"The Great Farini," Skull Boy explained. "He was a famous acrobat who crossed Niagara Falls on a tightrope and did all kinds of other seemingly impossible stunts. I've been researching famous stunt performers—acrobats, magicians, escape artists—to see if I can find some relation in my family tree. I guess I can rule out acrobats like the Great Farini, since I'm so clumsy." Skull Boy didn't know who his ancestors were, so he was always trying to guess.

"Did you guys see the rain yet?" he inquired. "What are we going to do inside all day?"

"I don't know," said Ruby, "but we've got a lot of ideas and I'm sure you do, too. Let's get everyone together and take a vote."

"Awesome," Skull Boy said, and they went downstairs. Everyone grabbed an umbrella from

the antique cast-iron umbrella stand next to the door, and they all went outside to Frank and Len's garage.

Frank and Len shared a lot of things—a passion for loud music, the same punk rock taste in clothes . . . and a body. For the most part, they worked in harmony—Frank wrote music in a notebook while Len picked out tunes on their guitar. Sometimes they had trouble understanding each other, as Len often took things too literally, but they always worked it out in the end. As Ruby, Iris, Skull Boy, Misery, and Doom Kitty approached the garage, they heard what sounded like a herd of roaring walruses coming from inside. They hurried to the door to see what was wrong.

"Hey, are you guys okay in there?" Ruby called, and knocked on the door.

Frank and Len answered the door with
innocent looks on their faces and said, "Yeah,
we're all right. What's going on, guys? Come in
out of the rain."

"Is your new pet walrus okay?" Iris asked
as she walked into the bedroom/music studio.
"Can I meet him? Maybe I can help."

"Um . . . who?" Frank asked, really confused
now.

"We don't have a new pet walrus," Len said,
"but we did just write a new song called 'Sea
Blubber.'
Wanna hear
it!'"

At this, the
gang laughed.
"Oh, so *that's*
what that
sound was.
Yeah, sure,

play it for us," Ruby said, and took a seat on the couch. Frank and Len picked up their guitar, turned their amplifier volume up to eleven, and began to jam. Sure enough, the sound was just like a herd of roaring walruses, and everyone clapped their hands and danced around the room to it. The brothers finished with one final roar of the guitar, and then took their bows to wild applause from their friends.

"Wow!" Iris said. "That reminded me of an adventure I once had exploring the ocean."

"That reminded me of cute little sea creatures playing," Ruby said.

"That reminded me of San Francisco," Misery said, ". . . during an earthquake."

"Thanks, guys," said Frank. "Hey—what are we going to do today? Any ideas?"

"Oh, yes, lots," Ruby said. "We just need to get Poe, Boo Boo, and Scaredy Bat together and then we can all make a plan."

Just as she spoke the words, Boo Boo flew through the door—as in, *through* the door. He was still a ghost-in-training, but he could move through solid objects. "Boo!" he shouted. Everyone looked up at him and smiled, much to his dismay. Boo Boo's greatest wish was to be frightening, but he had one major handicap— he was as cute as a puppy. Most people who saw him said, "Aww!" but he wanted them to scream, "Ahh!"

"Good morning, Boo Boo," Ruby greeted the chubby-cheeked ghost. "We were just about to

come looking for you. Have you seen Poe?"

"Yeah," Boo Boo said, disappointed that no one was scared upon his entrance. "He's right outside the door."

Iris crossed the room and opened the door. Poe stood there dripping with rain, but with just as much dignity as if he were standing in a balcony at the opera house.

He wore his usual formal black jacket and top hat. "Good morning," he said in his upper-crust accent. "Are the walruses all right?" And then he stepped stiffly inside.

Poe was a self-professed, refined, educated crow who lived with his brothers, Edgar and Allen, in a coop outside the mansion. The coop was filled with books and opera records, as Poe was a big fan of the arts. He even claimed to be descended from the great writer Edgar Allen Poe's pet budgie, Paco.

"Hey, Poe," Ruby said cheerfully, closing the door, "are you excited for our rainy day?"

"Indeed," Poe replied directly. "Rain is good for the soul. I always write my best poetry to the tap-tap-tapping of raindrops on my windowpane."

"Is that what we're going to do today?" Len asked. "Write poetry?"

"Well, maybe," said Ruby. "Let's go find Scaredy Bat and see what he wants to do."

The entire gang went back to the mansion and straight up to Scaredy Bat's room. They knew he would still be in his hammock, hiding under the covers. Scaredy Bat was often too afraid to get up, insisting there was a luna monster in the closet or a bogeyman under the bed. And on a day like today, with the thunder rumbling and lightning flashing across the sky, Scaredy Bat was sure to be very, very afraid . . .

Chapter Two

"Don't wish for courage—
wish for an opportunity
to be courageous!"

Ruby went to the tiny bat's room and tried to coax him out from under the covers. "Scaredy . . ." she called, "don't be afraid of the rain—we're going to stay indoors and play together all day. Doesn't that sound like fun?"

"Oh no, Ruby," Scaredy Bat said nervously from the deepest part of the hammock. "There are monsters out there today, I am sure of it. I just heard the sound of a herd of roaring walruses and I'm sure they're coming to get us!"

At this, everyone laughed—especially Frank and Len. "No, little dude," Frank said reassuringly, "that was just us, playing our new song."

Scaredy Bat poked his head up from under the blanket.

"Really?" Everyone nodded comfortingly. "Oh." Then Scaredy Bat turned to Ruby and asked, "Well . . . what are we going to play?"

"We don't know yet. We thought maybe you could help us decide. How about we all go downstairs and discuss it over some breakfast?" Ruby said. Scaredy Bat nodded slowly and climbed out of the hammock. Ruby picked him up, and they all went down together.

"I think we should build chair-skis and ride down the staircase in a great, big furniture Olympics!" Iris said energetically as she took a bun from a basket in the center of the table.

Everyone sat around the large, rectangular dining table in the dining room. The rain pattered against the floor-to-ceiling windows as they drank juice and ate breakfast. Scaredy Bat shivered nervously and dove underneath his seat every time the thunder clapped.

"Oh no, I'm afraid I could never participate in such an event," Scaredy Bat said from under his chair, nibbling on a lemon poppy-seed muffin. "Sporting events involving furniture are far too dangerous for a tiny bat like me."

"Okay. Wanna go bungee jumping off the banister?" Iris suggested. Scaredy gasped, horrified at the thought.

"How about we go outside and play Dodge the Lightning?" Misery suggested. Then she reconsidered. "Never mind—I always lose that game." She reached for the plate of buns, but it was empty. "Hmm," she noted, unsurprised.

"We could play hide and go seek," Skull Boy

suggested, cutting his muffin in half and sharing it with Misery.

"Oh no, I couldn't," Scaredy Bat answered. "I'm far too afraid of being lost and never getting found."

Even Doom Kitty put in her two cents. When

Ruby asked her what she'd like to do all day, she curled up into a ball, wrapped her tail around her head, and breathed deeply and evenly. Clearly, Doom Kitty wanted to take a catnap. She often communicated to Ruby and the gang through pantomime. Trouble was, everyone except Ruby had difficulty understanding her.

"No, we can't sleep all day, Doom," Ruby said. "Then what would we do all night? Today is a perfect day to try something new!" Doom sighed—she was perfectly content to do something new in her dreams.

"Well, I, for one, would like to spend the day writing poetry. I've been reading the greats all week and I am inspired," Poe stated.

"Oh no, no, no, I couldn't," Scaredy Bat said anxiously. "I don't have the talent for that, no."

"Talent!" Ruby shouted. "That's it!" Everyone looked at her curiously. "Let's have a talent show!"

"Yeah!" Iris agreed. "Let's have it right here in the Great Hall! I'll do my trapeze act!"

"Okay!" Frank and Len said. "We can perform a new song!"

"I know what I'm going to do," Ruby said eagerly. "Sew some new sock puppets and put on a puppet show with Mr. Buns!"

"I think I'll try my hand at some sort of magic act," Skull Boy said thoughtfully. "I may not be related to the Great Farini, but it is possible I am descended from the Great Harry

Houdini. He could do everything from simple card tricks to elaborate escape acts. Maybe I have inherited some of his talent."

Poe added, "I shall recite some very profound, elegant, beautiful poetry to stir the soul and stimulate the mind of my audience."

"We can't wait to hear it, Poe," Ruby interrupted, "but save it for the talent show. What will you do, Misery?"

She looked up and said directly, "Comedy." Ruby raised an eyebrow. "Comedy?" she asked. "You . . . can do . . . I mean, what kind of . . . ?"

Misery noticed that everyone looked rather surprised. "What? I'm a riot," she stated matter-of-factly. "My third cousin started a riot once, but no one laughed . . . I'm not sure why."

"Oh my, oh my," Scaredy Bat cut in. He was pacing the length of the dining room, holding his head in his wings. "I'm afraid I cannot participate in this talent show," he cried.

"Why not?" Iris asked.

"Not only do I not have any special talent," Scaredy moaned, "but I also have terrible, terrible stage fright!"

"Aw, Scaredy, I'm sure if you give it some thought, you can come up with an act," Ruby said positively. "Just spend some quiet time by yourself and try to think of something. Here— take Mr. Buns with you if you don't want to be alone. I don't need him yet, anyway. I've got lots of sock puppets to sew."

Ruby pulled a black sock puppet with a white face and a red nose out of her pocket. Mr. Buns had two floppy ears, and was something of a mystery to all the friends in the mansion. He didn't talk or move, but always somehow managed to go from one part of the mansion to another, quite unexpectedly. He was a good friend, though, and Ruby loved him.

Scaredy Bat took the sock puppet and hugged it. "Oh, I must think of something," he lamented. "But how, what . . ."

"Hey, Scaredy," Skull Boy said, "I'm really going to need an assistant for my magic act. How about helping me out?"

"Are . . . are you certain it will be safe?" Scaredy Bat hesitated.

"Totally," Skull Boy reassured him. "There isn't really any such thing as magic—all the tricks are performed with sleight of hand. Come on, I'll show you."

One by one, each of the friends dashed off to their rooms to rehearse their acts for the big show. "Oh dear, oh dear," Scaredy Bat said, following Skull Boy up to his room, still a little uneasy. He held tightly to Mr. Buns, trying to muster his courage.

Chapter Three

"In every performance,
there is a little bit of magic
. . . and a lot of practice!"

Skull Boy and Scaredy Bat spent an hour
rummaging through the attic, searching for
props. They found an old magician's chest
containing a deck of cards, a top hat, a black
magician's cape, and a
magic wand for Skull
Boy. They also found a
nice magician's assistant
costume for Scaredy
Bat to wear—a robe
covered in shiny purple
sequins. The two friends

carried the props and costumes down to the Great Hall for a practice session.

"Okay," Skull Boy said, fanning out the deck of cards and holding them forth, "pick a card, any card." Scaredy Bat carefully selected a card and pulled it out of the deck. He looked at it, showed it to Mr. Buns, then held it facedown so Skull Boy couldn't see.

"I shall now use my magical powers to read your mind and discover that the card you selected is . . ." Skull Boy paused for dramatic effect, and then said in a booming voice, "The jack of diamonds!"

Scaredy Bat stared up at Skull Boy. Then he glanced back down at his card. Sheepishly, he looked up again and shook his head. "No."

"Oh—the thunderstorm must have interfered with the connection between our minds. I shall read your mind again, stronger now, and guess that your card is . . . the ace of spades!" Skull

Boy pointed at the card, as if accusing it of some crime.

Scaredy Bat cleared his throat and looked nervously about the room. "Um, no, sir, it is not the ace of spades. I'm afraid the trick is not working proper—"

"Silence!" Skull Boy insisted. "I have it now! It is the three of hearts!"

"No."

"Six of clubs?" Skull Boy tried again.

"No."

"I'm sensing that it's a red card. Definitely red, am I right?"

"No, I'm afraid not," Scaredy Bat said. He turned his card over and revealed it to be the two of spades.

"Oh." Skull Boy sighed deeply. "Well, maybe card tricks aren't my strength. Let's try something else. How about a disappearing act!"

"Oh my goodness," Scaredy Bat said

worriedly. "I do not like the sound of that."

"Come on, it'll be okay. My ancestors used to do this all the time . . . I think." Skull Boy led Scaredy Bat over to the coat closet near the staircase and opened the door. "Now, you hop in the magic closet, then I'll say the magic words, and you'll disappear. Then I'll say some more magic words, and you'll reappear. There's nothing to it!"

Scaredy Bat shook as he stepped toward the closet, holding Mr. Buns close. Skull Boy closed the door and then tapped the top of it three times with his magic wand. Then he tapped the sides three times as well, saying, "Hey hocus-pocus, hey nonny non, alakazam, make Scaredy gone!" Then he opened the closet door and . . . Scaredy Bat was gone!

Skull Boy poked his head all the way into the dark closet. He looked down, side to side, and up. He kept searching until he was absolutely certain that Scaredy Bat was nowhere inside that closet. *Wow!* Skull Boy thought. *I'm better than I thought! I guess magic really does run in my family! I'd better bring him back now though, just to be safe.*

So once again, Skull Boy closed the closet door, tapped it three times with his magic wand, and said the magic words. "Abracadabra, walla walla wack, goochie goochie goo, bring Scaredy Bat back!" Then he swung open the closet door and looked inside. Only . . . Scaredy Bat still was not there.

Again, Skull Boy closed the door and said the magic words, and again, the closet remained empty. He was starting to worry. He tried different magic words, banging on the walls of the closet, tried it all again with the magician's cape and hat on, but nothing worked. Scaredy Bat had vanished and now Skull Boy didn't know how to make him reappear! *I've got to get the others!* he decided. *Maybe they can help me figure out what I'm doing wrong.*

He rushed off to find Ruby, and wondered how he was going to explain that he had just lost one of their best friends.

Chapter Four

"Now you see it, now you
don't . . . but that doesn't mean
you ever give up searching!"

When Skull Boy burst through Ruby's door,
she was hard at work in front of her sewing
machine, surrounded by odd socks in vibrant
colors as well as buttons, needles, pins, and

thread. "Ruby,
come quick!"
he panted, out
of breath from
running up
the stairs and
down the hall
so fast.

"What's wrong?" Ruby asked, alarmed.

"It's Scaredy Bat. He . . . he disappeared!" Skull Boy said frantically. "I don't know how I did it, but I made him disappear! I put him in the closet, said the magic words, and I didn't think it would work but it did and now he's gone!"

Ruby took a deep breath and told Skull Boy to do the same. "Calm down," she said. "I'm sure there's a perfectly reasonable explanation for this. Maybe he was so scared to be shut inside a dark closet that he slipped out before you even shut the door. Did you double-check that he was even in there before you said the magic words?"

"Yes, yes, I'm sure of it," Skull Boy said. "Ruby, I know it sounds crazy, but I really think I made Scaredy Bat disappear!" Ruby thought for a moment. She was sure that if they just looked hard enough, they would find Scaredy

Bat hiding in one of his favorite spots behind the curtains, under the rug, or maybe even all the way back up in his room and in bed.

But after searching both the Great Hall and Scaredy Bat's room top to bottom, inside and out, they found nothing. "See? I told you," Skull Boy said. "Now do you believe me?"

"Nope," Ruby giggled. "Bats don't just disappear. I'm sure he ran off to join one of the others. Let's go ask around and check if anyone's seen him."

"I sure hope you're right," Skull Boy said, and followed Ruby down the hall to Iris's room.

"Come in!" Iris called when she heard the knock at the door. She was practicing her somersaults and split leaps on her trampoline, and did a triple back layout as Ruby and Skull Boy entered.

"Wow! You're getting really good at those," Ruby said.

"Thanks!" Iris answered. "You guys all ready for the talent show? Skull Boy, I'm really excited to see your magic act."

"Actually, well, funny you should mention the magic act. Uh . . ." Skull Boy stammered.

"Have you seen Scaredy Bat, by any chance?" Ruby asked. "He was with Skull Boy practicing a disappearing act, and suddenly he just sort of . . . well, let's just say he's missing. We were wondering if he came up here to join you."

Iris continued to practice on the trampoline and spoke between flips. "I'm sure . . . he just . . . ran off . . . because . . . he was . . . too scared," she said as she performed a double twist. "Don't worry . . . he'll turn up."

Ruby and Skull Boy decided to go check with Frank and Len at the garage.

The brothers were jamming at top volume when Ruby and Skull Boy walked in. Ruby shouted as loud as she could, but Frank and Len couldn't hear her over the music. She tried again, but the brothers just kept looking at her and mouthing, "What?" Finally, Skull Boy unplugged the amplifier.

"I SAID—" Ruby started to shout, but then realized the music was silenced. "I said," she repeated calmly, "have either of you seen Scaredy Bat recently? He seems to be missing."

"Disappeared," Skull Boy corrected.

"Whoa," Frank said, "like, *disappeared*

disappeared?" Skull Boy nodded, but Ruby shook her head. The brothers didn't know whom to believe.

Ruby clarified, "Skull Boy thinks he made Scaredy Bat disappear while practicing his magic act. I've been trying to tell him that it's more likely that Scaredy is hiding. So we were wondering if you have seen him."

"Cool!" Len said. "I want to disappear! Skull Boy, do it to me!"

"Not cool," Frank argued. "Len, the guy disappeared. Vanished. Went kaput. Gone fishing. Out to lunch. We haven't seen him, Ruby."

"First of all, he didn't disappear," Ruby tried to interrupt.

"Hey, I like fishing," Len said.

"No, it's a figure of speech," Frank argued.

"No one went out to lunch," Ruby tried again.

"No?" Len asked. "Then they must be hungry. Who's up for some franks and beans?" Ruby sighed and looked to Skull Boy. While Frank continued to try to explain the situation to Len, Ruby and Skull Boy slipped out the front door.

Ruby thought it would be a good idea to question Boo Boo, since he knew all of Scaredy Bat's hiding places. But after searching inside all of the cabinets, behind all the doors, and underneath all the beds, Boo Boo met Ruby and Skull Boy back in the Great Hall empty-handed.

Misery came down from her room to ask what all the fuss was about and, in her own special way, tried to console Skull Boy. "Don't feel bad," she said. "One of my ancestors was a magician's assistant, and she disappeared once, too."

"Did they find her?" Skull Boy asked hopefully.

After a pause, Misery said, "No."

Skull Boy was really starting to panic.

"Well, maybe we should just wait for him. I'm sure he'll come out when he's ready," Ruby said confidently. "Misery, why don't you practice some of your jokes on us while we wait?"

"Okay," said the tired-looking girl, "what's green and green and green and green and green?"

"A pickle rolling downhill," Skull Boy answered, checking under the rug for signs of Scaredy Bat. "Sorry—I've heard that one before."

"Nope," Misery answered. "That's not it. It's my great-great-great cousin Mortala after she accidentally ate arsenic and fell unconscious down the house stairs."

"Well, I hadn't heard it told that way before,"

Skullboy said. "Tell another one."

"Okay." Misery sighed. "Knock knock."

"Who's there?" Ruby responded.

"Boo."

"Nuh-uh—I'm over here," Boo Boo called from the top of the bookshelf, where he hovered above the group.

"No," Misery said, "it's part of the joke. Boo."

"What?" asked Boo.

"No, I'm saying 'Boo,'" Misery clarified.

"Are you trying to scare me?" Boo Boo asked, really confused this time.

Misery turned back to Ruby and Skull Boy. "Never mind," she said, and trudged off toward her staircase.

The friends waited together for a long while, listening to the rain, but there was no sign of Scaredy Bat anywhere. With each minute that passed, Skull Boy became more and more convinced that it was really magic.

Chapter Five

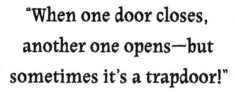

"When one door closes,
another one opens—but
sometimes it's a trapdoor!"

Standing in the dark closet, clutching Mr. Buns to his chest, Scaredy Bat heard Skull Boy chant the magic words "Hey hocus pocus, hey nonny non, alakazam, make Scaredy gone!" Then he heard three taps on the door, then another three on the right, and another three on the —"Whooooaaa!"

Suddenly, the floor gave way beneath Scaredy's feet and he dropped right through! He landed about ten feet below onto a dirt floor—*foomp*!

"AHH! AHH! AHH! AHH!" Scaredy Bat screamed over and over again, until he realized that he was all right. Nothing was broken. He was on a floor under the mansion, with gray stone walls forming tunnels that stretched off to the left and right. He was a little dirty, but otherwise intact. Mr. Buns had also survived the fall with nothing but a dirt smudge on his ear. Scaredy Bat sighed with relief. But where was he, exactly? What happened in the closet? How was he going to get back?

Scaredy Bat looked up nervously and examined the ceiling. He saw the outline of a square hatch, and figured that must be where he fell through. "A trapdoor!" he said. When Skull Boy tapped the left side of the closet, he must have tripped a lever and opened the hatch, sending Scaredy Bat and Mr. Buns down below. It was a very clever trick. *But how ever am I going to get back up there?* Scaredy Bat wondered. Then he heard Skull Boy calling for him.

"Scaredy? Scaredy Bat?" he called, confused. "Hocus-pocus? Yabba daba? . . . Hello? Scaredy, where are you?" At this, Scaredy Bat realized that Skull Boy *didn't know* about the trapdoor. This was all an accident!

"Hello! I'm down here!" Scaredy Bat called up toward the ceiling. But his voice was so soft that it was drowned out by the thunder and rain. Scaredy Bat called and called, but it was no use. Skull Boy couldn't hear him.

"Oh no!" Scaredy Bat said to Mr. Buns. "I'm afraid we are trapped down here!" Scaredy looked down to where Mr. Buns had fallen, but he wasn't there. He looked around, and found Mr. Buns about eight feet away, near the mouth of one of the tunnels. Scaredy Bat looked down the tunnel as far as he could see, which wasn't very far at all, given that there wasn't much light. "Do you think it will lead us to a way out?" Scaredy Bat wondered out loud. Mr. Buns didn't answer, but one of his arms did seem to be pointing farther into the tunnel.

"Well, I suppose we have no choice but to follow the path. I do hope there are no scary monsters living under the mansion," Scaredy Bat said nervously as he took a step forward. He picked up Mr. Buns and took another step. Then another.

"Well, this isn't so very difficult, I've already taken—AAAAHHHHHH!" Scaredy Bat screamed. "A monster! A monster!" He cowered up against the wall and shivered with fright. After a few seconds, though, he realized there was still no one in the tunnel except himself and Mr. Buns. "Where did the monster go?" Scaredy asked, standing up and peering down the tunnel. Mr. Buns didn't answer, but his head seemed to be turned toward the floor. Scaredy Bat looked down and saw his large shadow stretched forward on the ground. That was the "monster" that had scared him so.

"It is very silly of me, I suppose," Scaredy Bat said, trying to sound brave as he picked up Mr. Buns, "to be afraid of my own shadow. I will try to keep my wits about me from now on, Mr. Buns, or I fear we'll never get out of here."

Mr. Buns rested comfortably in Scaredy Bat's arms as they ventured forward into the long, dark tunnel together.

Meanwhile, upstairs in the Great Hall, Ruby, Iris, Misery, Skull Boy, Frank and Len, Poe, and

Boo Boo continued to try to solve the mystery of Scaredy Bat's disappearance. While they discussed the situation, Doom Kitty inspected the closet.

"I'm telling you, it's magic," Skull Boy insisted. "If I can just find some of the old books in the library, I'm sure I can find the right set of magic words to bring Scaredy back."

"Skull Boy," Ruby said with assurance, "I'm sure you are a very talented magician and that your act for the talent show is first-rate, but it is far more likely that Scaredy Bat is just lost right now, and didn't disappear at all."

"I don't know, Ruby," Iris said, "we've looked everywhere in the mansion and he still hasn't turned up. Maybe he really did disappear."

"Yeah, 'gone fishing,'" Len chimed in.

"Well, I'm going to go check the garden," Ruby said. "You all keep looking."

Just as Ruby left the room, Doom Kitty

stumbled over something on the side of the closet. It was a lever, and when she nuzzled it, she saw the trapdoor open on the inside! She ran to tell Skull Boy, bounding over to where he sat, rubbing up hard against his legs.

"What is it, Doom?" Skull Boy asked. Doom Kitty traced a tall rectangle in the air, and then pretended to open it like a door. She tapped the side of the rectangle, then stepped inside and collapsed, as though the floor had just fallen out from under her.

"Are you feeling faint?" Skull Boy asked. "I can get you some water." Doom Kitty shook her head. She started the pantomime again, and all the friends gathered around to try to figure out her message.

She traced the tall rectangle again, and then stepped inside and outside to show that it was a door. She tapped the side, jumped in, and fell down. She even pointed toward the closet, to try

to get them to go over there and see what she
was talking about.

"She's pointing toward the
stairs," Skull Boy noted.

"You jumped on the
stairs and fell down?" Frank
guessed.

"You want to go chair-
skiing down the stairs with
me?" Iris tried.

"We don't have time for
chair-skiing right now, Doom," Len said. "We've
got to find Scaredy Bat." Doom Kitty slapped
her paw against her forehead while the others
walked off to search the mansion once again for
their missing friend.

Chapter Six

> "Don't be afraid of shadows. Shadows mean there's a light nearby!"

Scaredy Bat moved slowly and cautiously through the tunnel. Above him were the floorboards of the mansion, and light shone down through the cracks, making it easier to see where he was going. He could hear the footsteps and voices of his friends calling for him. Once in a while he would try to call back to them, but he was too far below the floor for them to hear him up above.

Scaredy Bat was about as scared as he had ever been in his life. Every sound was cause for alarm. He worried about anything and everything that could possibly happen, like falling through another trapdoor, or getting even more lost and never getting found, or meeting snakes or monsters. His heart raced as he sped up his footsteps.

At one point, Scaredy was convinced he was being followed. Every time he took a step he would hear a dragging noise behind him. But when he turned around, there was no one there. He stopped, listened, and then took another step. The noise returned. He stopped again and listened, but it was silent. No one was behind him. Scaredy stood still for a minute. He was scared to move forward, but he was also scared to stand there in the dark waiting. Finally he took a deep breath and decided to take a step in slow motion and then turn around quickly, to try to catch the culprit in the act. He closed his eyes and thought, *One, two . . . THREE!* and he wheeled around to look behind him. As he turned, however, his feet got caught in the long, purple, sequined robe that dragged behind him, and he tripped. "Ahh!" he screamed, trying to untangle himself. When he finally smoothed out his robe, he realized he and Mr. Buns were still alone. That's when he figured it out. "There is no one following us, Mr. Buns," he told his friend, giggling nervously. "The dragging sound was just my costume." Scaredy Bat smiled. It was kind of funny, now that he thought about it. He picked himself up and continued through the passageway.

He eventually came to a fork in the tunnel— one path continued straight and the other path veered

to the left. "Uh-oh," Scaredy said, "I do not know which way to go." He placed Mr. Buns next to a rock on the floor and looked at his options.

While he sat there, thinking it over, he heard all sorts of scary sounds in the tunnels around him. He heard bumps, thuds, squeaks, and creaks. Scaredy Bat shivered with fear. "Oh dear, oh dear, oh dear. There are monsters down here, I know it!"

But then Scaredy Bat saw that the squeaks were just a friendly little mouse scurrying by. The thuds were water droplets hitting the ground from overhead; they must have trickled down all the way from the leak in Misery's room. The creaks were just the floorboards overhead, and as for the bumps? "Well," Scaredy said, "everyone always says to beware of things that go bump in the night. But Ruby says things that go bump in the daytime are usually friendly. So it is probably okay. Right, Mr. Buns?" Scaredy looked toward the rock where he had left—or rather, where he thought he had left—his friend. But Mr. Buns was not there.

Scaredy Bat rose to his feet and looked around timidly. He hoped Mr. Buns hadn't been kidnapped by the bogeyman! Luckily Mr. Buns was waiting patiently on the floor of the tunnel that veered toward the left. "Is this the way out of here, Mr. Buns?" Scaredy asked. "Is that what you are trying to tell me? All right, then, you lead the way."

From that moment on, every time Scaredy Bat came to a fork in the tunnel, he let Mr. Buns choose which direction to take. Not only that, but every time he encountered something scary, he tried to think of one of Ruby's sayings. Somehow, they made him feel better. When he thought he heard the bogeyman again, he thought of how Ruby always said, "The bogeyman lives in the dark, so turn off the light and get to know him!" If Ruby thought the bogeyman was worth knowing, then he probably wasn't as frightening as Scaredy thought! And when he saw some cobwebs, he thought of how Ruby always said, "Spiders keep the bugs out!" And it was true—Scaredy hadn't seen any bugs, which was good because some bugs were scary!

Eventually, Scaredy Bat started to think that the tunnel wasn't so bad. It could have been worse. After all, he was very afraid of heights and so far he hadn't encountered any—

"Oh no!" Scaredy Bat gasped as he turned the corner and saw where the tunnel had taken him. He found himself inside a circular room— with one smooth, stone wall all around—and there were no tunnels or pathways branching off of it. There was only one way to continue on, and that was . . . up. There were iron rungs built into the wall that formed a ladder. The ladder went up, up, up, and Scaredy could see the rainy sky way up at the top. Water trickled down from the hole. It was then that he realized where he was.

"Mr. Buns, we are at the bottom of the well in the garden outside the mansion. If we can just make it up to the top of this ladder, we'll be home," Scaredy said. He was relieved to have finally found an exit from the tunnel underneath the house, but he was also very frightened of climbing up the ladder. Scaredy Bat was horribly afraid of heights. In fact, he was so afraid of heights that he, unlike most bats, didn't even like to fly!

"I do not know how I am ever going to get up to the top. What if I fall off? What if I look down and get dizzy? What if I get stuck in the middle and can't make it the rest of the way? Oh, woe is me, woe is me . . ."

Scaredy Bat started to cry, which is a normal

thing to do when you're afraid, but then he remembered something that Ruby had once said: "The first step is the hardest, but it's easier with a friend." So he took Mr. Buns by the hand, and placed his foot on the first rung of the ladder.

Chapter Seven

"Magic is believing in yourself!"

The afternoon wore on and the rain never let up. Ruby and her friends redoubled their efforts and searched the mansion again. Skull Boy even went upstairs to put his magic wand away in the attic, lest he make anyone else disappear or accidentally conjure up a luna monster.

"I guess this proves that I really am descended from a great magician," he said with a sigh as he opened the magician's chest. "Somehow, I thought I would feel happier about it." He contemplated the wand before laying it in the chest and said, "I suppose I could give

it one more shot.
Abracadabra, walla
walla wack, goochie
goochie gooo, bring
Scaredy back!"

Ruby and Doom
Kitty sat by the window,
listening to Skull Boy and
watching the rain. Ruby was about to tell Skull
Boy once and for all that it wasn't magic that
made Scaredy Bat disappear, but suddenly Doom
Kitty jumped up and pointed urgently out the
window. "What is it, Doom?" Ruby asked. Doom
Kitty jumped on Ruby's shoulder and pointed
her paw straight out the window. Ruby looked
and saw . . . could it be? Yes—it was Scaredy
Bat!

"Scaredy Bat is back!" Ruby shouted with
glee. Skull Boy rushed over and saw him, too,
right there in the middle of the garden.

"Wow! I did it!" He clapped his hands with excitement and relief. The three of them ran down the stairs calling, "Scaredy's back! Scaredy's back! Come quick!" so that everyone would stop searching. Everyone met at the front door and grabbed their umbrellas. They took an extra one for Scaredy Bat, and went out to meet him in the garden.

Scaredy Bat was getting drenched by the heavy rain, but even though the thunder sounded loudly in the sky, he wasn't afraid. He was too happy to be frightened.

"Hello, my friends! I am so happy to see you!" he cried, and everyone gathered around for a big group hug. Frank and Len held an umbrella over Scaredy Bat's head while the gang walked back inside.

Ruby made some hot cocoa, and Iris brought out a couple of warm towels for both Scaredy Bat and Mr. Buns. Once they were both safe and warm, Skull Boy asked, "So, what was it like to disappear? Where did you go, exactly?"

"Yeah," Len added, "did you go out to lunch?" Frank rolled his eyes. Scaredy Bat giggled at the questions.

"Oh no, it was nothing like that," he said. "There is a trapdoor beneath the closet. When Mr. Skull Boy tapped the side of the closet three times with his magic wand, it tripped a lever and opened the hatch. I tumbled right through and landed in a secret passageway that runs underneath the entire house. Luckily, Mr. Buns was with me and helped me find my way out."

All the friends paused for a moment at the idea that Mr. Buns could direct Scaredy Bat out of the underground tunnel. But they had each experienced some pretty strange things whenever Mr. Buns was around, so they accepted Scaredy Bat's explanation. Ruby walked over to the closet in the Great Hall and examined the floor. Sure enough, the trapdoor opened and closed every time she tapped the left side of the door.

"That's what Doom Kitty was trying to tell us all along," she realized, and reached down to pet her head. Doom rubbed up against Ruby's ankles, purring.

Iris turned to Scaredy Bat and asked, "So, what's it like down in those tunnels? You must have had a wonderful adventure!"

"It was terrifying!" Scaredy Bat replied. "It was dark and the walls were gray and cold. I tried to call out to you, but no one could hear me, so I looked for a way out." Everyone's attention was fixed on Scaredy Bat.

"I thought someone was following me, but it turned out to be my costume," Scaredy Bat continued. "I thought

I saw the bogeyman, but it was just my own shadow."

"What was the scariest part of all?" Misery asked.

"The last part, most definitely," Scaredy Bat replied, "when I had to climb the steepest, tallest ladder to get out of the well. I'm afraid of heights, you know."

"We know," Ruby said, impressed by Scaredy Bat's bravery. "We're all just so glad you're okay."

"And I'm just so glad I didn't make you vanish into thin air!" Skull Boy added.

"I say," Poe suggested, "now that we're all gathered here, wouldn't it be an excellent time to present our talent show?"

Everyone jumped to their feet enthusiastically and said, "Yeah, let's do it!"

"Oh no, no, no, no, no," Scaredy Bat said, shaking his head and hiding his face inside his blanket.

"What's wrong, Scaredy?" Boo Boo asked.

"I'm afraid I still don't have a talent to share with the group, and I'm still very afraid of being onstage," he replied.

"But you're so brave!" Boo Boo argued.

"What?" Scaredy Bat said, shocked. No one had ever called him brave before.

"Yeah. You just fell through a trapdoor and landed in a dark, scary tunnel," Iris explained. "You had to face the dark, strange noises, your fear of heights, and even your fear of getting lost and never getting found. Somehow, you faced all those fears and found your way out, anyway!"

"But I was terrified, horrified, petrified! I was scared the whole way through!" Scaredy Bat said, still hiding his face in the blanket.

"Yes, you were. But Scaredy," Ruby said, kneeling down in front of him, "being brave doesn't mean you're never afraid. Being brave means you are afraid but you push forward, anyway." Scaredy Bat looked up at Ruby and smiled.

"I suppose after walking through all those dark tunnels," Poe added, "getting up on a brightly lit stage in front of your dearest friends shouldn't be too difficult a thing."

Scaredy Bat nodded and smiled. He would give it his best try.

Chapter Eight

"Talent is helpful, but guts
are more important!"

Ruby sewed some red curtains and hung
them up in front of a raised wooden platform
in the Great Hall. Skull Boy found an old
microphone and set it up. Frank and Len then
plugged the microphone into their amplifier. Poe
set up some chairs in front of the stage, and all
the friends took a seat. When the spotlights were
on and the stage was set, Boo Boo
swooped in and announced into
the microphone, "Good evening,
ladies and germs!"

Ruby, Skull Boy, Poe, Doom

Kitty, Iris, Frank and Len, and Scaredy Bat applauded. Even Poe's brothers Edgar and Allen, had come in to see the show, so the hall was quite full.

"Welcome to the Rainy Day Talent Show! We've got a great show for you tonight, featuring Iris on the flying trapeze, Ruby and Doom Kitty and their amazing sock puppet friends, Frank and Len's new song, 'Hiss Kiss,' Poe's poetry, Misery's comedy act, and the Great Skulldini, and his assistant, Scaredy Bat!" The whole audience clapped.

"And now," Boo Boo said with a wave of his arm, "without further ado, Iris on the flying trapeze!" Iris jumped up from her seat, wearing a glittery red leotard and a feather in her hair. She climbed up to a trapeze swing that had been hooked into the ceiling. She smiled to the audience, and then leaped onto the swing.

Back and forth she swung, doing flips

and turns in the air. The acrobatics grew more complex as she swung, until with one final triple twist backward layout quadruple flip, she missed the bar of

the trapeze swing and crash-landed into the bookcase. Everyone gasped but Iris quickly called out, "I'm good!"

"Let's hear it for Iris. Wasn't she terrific?" Boo Boo said, clapping his hands encouragingly. Wild applause erupted from the audience. Iris stood up, curtsied to the audience, and went back to her seat.

Boo Boo continued the show. "Next, put your hands together for Ruby, Doom Kitty, and their amazing sock puppets!" During the applause, Ruby and Doom Kitty set up a small sock puppet theater. Ruby put Mr. Buns on one hand, and a new puppet, Mrs. Buns, on another hand. Doom

Kitty put a sock puppet with a mustache on the end of her tail. This was the Evil Landlord.

"You must pay the rent!" Ruby said in a manly voice, while Doom Kitty moved the mouth of the Evil Landlord puppet.

Ruby then moved the mouth of Mrs. Buns and said in a high-pitched voice, "But I can't pay the rent!"

The Evil Landlord shouted again, "Pay the rent!"

And Mrs. Buns replied, "But I can't pay the rent!"

A third time, the Evil Landlord demanded, "Pay the rent!" The audience looked worried—would Mrs. Buns be able to pay the rent?

"But I can't pay the rent!" she cried. Just then, Mr. Buns heroically burst onto the stage on Ruby's other hand.

"I'll pay the rent!" Ruby said in a friendly man's voice. Mrs. Buns sighed and swooned.

"My hero!" she said. Then Mr. and Mrs. Buns embraced, and the Evil Landlord left them alone.

"The end!" Ruby announced, and she and Doom Kitty bowed to applause from the audience.

Next, Frank and Len played their new song, "Hiss Kiss." It sounded like, well, a bunch of cats—lots of hissing and scratching. The audience loved it!

Poe took the stage next, and really surprised everyone. They were expecting him to recite a long, drawn-out poem with lots of big words. But instead he took the stage and said merely, "This haiku is entitled, 'Rain.'" He paused for a few moments, and then said,

"A pond, warm in spring—
the sound of a frog jumping
into the water."

Then there was silence while he stood on

the stage, perfectly still, looking very thoughtful. Then he dropped his head and the spotlight went out. The audience applauded politely.

Poe bowed deeply and took his seat between Edgar and Allen. "The genius is in what the author *doesn't* say," he commented. The brothers nodded approvingly.

Boo Boo took the stage again and said, "Thank you, Poe. And now I'd like to turn everyone's attention to center stage, for the comic stylings of . . . Misery!" Misery rose from her seat and dragged a large black sack up onto the stage with her. She stopped front and center and looked at the audience with her usual deadpan expression.

She reached inside her bag and pulled out a rubber chicken. She held it up for all to see, but said nothing. Then she reached inside her bag and pulled out a banana. She peeled the banana carefully, placed the fruit back in the bag, and then put the peel on the floor to the right. The last item she pulled out of the black sack was a pie, piled high with whipped cream.

Holding the rubber chicken in one hand and the pie in the other, Misery turned to the right and began to walk.
When she reached
the banana peel,
she stepped on it,
slipped, and fell. As
she fell to the floor,
she lost control of
the chicken and the
pie. Both flew up into the air, and the pie landed smack-dab on top of her head. Misery sat still, and waited for her applause.

Ruby, Skull Boy, and the gang watched Misery in silence at first, but seeing her there covered in whipped cream, knowing she planned to do it all along, was just too funny. Ruby giggled first. Then Skull Boy and Iris started to laugh, too. Scaredy Bat and Frank and Len joined in, and even Poe couldn't keep it inside. Soon everybody was having a great, big belly laugh, and they gave Misery a big round of applause.

Misery stood, bowed, and returned to her seat, never changing expression.

Boo Boo returned to the stage. "I would now like to introduce the Great—"

Before he could finish, Skull Boy rushed up onto the stage and whispered something in Boo Boo's ear. Boo Boo nodded and gave Skull Boy a wink and a thumbs-up sign.

"Ahem," he continued. "Ladies and gentlemen, we have a change in the performance schedule. Instead of the Great Skulldini and his assistant Scaredy Bat, we are going to see . . . the Great Scaredini and his assistant Skull Boy!"

"Huh?" Frank said.

"Well, this is a surprise," Ruby said.

Skull Boy took the stage first and said, "Hello, everyone. By now you have all heard about Scaredy Bat's courageous adventure through the tunnels below the mansion, right?" The audience nodded enthusiastically. "Now I would like to invite you to witness this daredevil bat's bravery firsthand! He is going to perform for you a series of very brave stunts, starting with . . . may I have a drumroll, please?"

Frank and Len quickly picked up a pair of drumsticks and played a roll on the floor. Skull Boy continued, "Getting up on the stage!"

Frank and Len pounded the floor with their drumsticks in a dramatic *ba dum pum* while Scaredy Bat slowly, nervously stepped up onto the stage and into the spotlight. His heart was pounding out of his chest with fear, but he did it. The audience erupted in lively applause.

"Yay, Scaredy!" they shouted.

"But wait, there's more!" Skull Boy announced. "For his next feat of bravery, we will turn out the spotlight and Scaredy Bat will stand up here, in the dark, without hiding, for five . . . whole . . . seconds!" The audience gasped. They had never seen Scaredy do anything like that in his life. He was terrified of the dark!

But sure enough, when Frank and Len played the drumroll, the lights went out and Scaredy Bat did not move. He did shut his eyes tight and whisper, "Oh dear, oh dear," until it was over. When the lights came back on, he was still there, shivering with fear. He hadn't run off to hide. He had faced his fear and won.

His friends went wild with delight. They clapped, hooted, and hollered. As Scaredy Bat rejoined his friends in the audience, he was given lots of pats on the back and high fives.

After the show everyone met in the kitchen for some lemon cookies and punch. They were all sure that the Rainy Day Talent Show was the best talent show that Gloomsville had ever seen.

"So," Iris asked, "should we start calling you Bravey Bat?"

Scaredy Bat opened his mouth to answer, but suddenly lightning flashed outside and a roar of thunder boomed and echoed through the house. Scaredy Bat dove under the rug and trembled, calling out, "Tell me when it's over!"

"Scaredy Bat, it is!" Iris confirmed, and all the friends laughed as another fun-filled day came to an end.

Dear Friend,

Were you as impressed as I was that Scaredy Bat was able to face his fears like that? It's amazing how such a tiny bat could have such a big heart. It just goes to show that no tunnel is too dark or too scary when you know a friend is waiting for you at the end.

Well, that's it for now. But don't worry. My friends and I have many more adventures that we want to share with you.

Like I always say, it's always best to face your fears before your fears face you!

Your friend,

Ruby

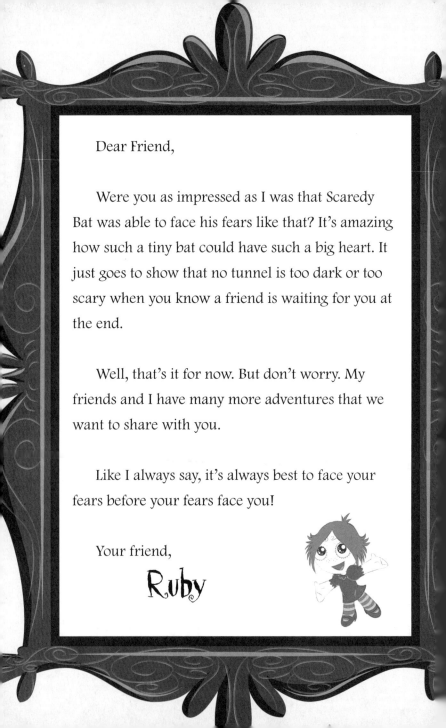